Paul & Emma Rogers

The Brave Little Hedgehog

PUFFIN

There was once a little hedgehog
who loved listening to stories.
   "I wish I could be in
a story," he said.

The Brave Little Hedgehog

For Jacob

PUFFIN BOOKS

Published by the Penguin Group
Penguin Books Ltd, 80 Strand, London WC2R 0RL, England
Penguin Group (USA), Inc., 375 Hudson Street, New York, New York 10014, USA
Penguin Books Australia Ltd, 250 Camberwell Road, Camberwell, Victoria 3124, Australia
Penguin Books Canada Ltd, 10 Alcorn Avenue, Toronto, Ontario, Canada M4V 3B2
Penguin Books India (P) Ltd, 11 Community Centre, Panchsheel Park, New Delhi – 110 017, India
Penguin Group (NZ), cnr Airborne and Rosedale Roads, Albany, Auckland 1310, New Zealand
Penguin Books (South Africa) (Pty) Ltd, 24 Sturdee Avenue, Rosebank 2196, South Africa

Penguin Books Ltd, Registered Offices: 80 Strand, London WC2R 0RL, England

www.penguin.com

Published 2005
1 3 5 7 9 10 8 6 4 2

Copyright © Paul and Emma Rogers, 2005
All rights reserved

The moral right of the author and illustrator has been asserted

Set in Lomba

Manufactured in China

British Library Cataloguing in Publication Data
A CIP catalogue record for this book is available from the British Library

ISBN 0–140–56939–1

So, the next day
he set off to try his luck.

Before long the little hedgehog met...
three little pigs!
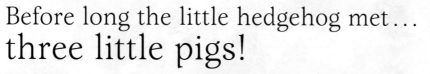
  "Not *just* three little pigs," they
told him. "*THE* three little pigs."
  "What! The ones in the story?"
said the little hedgehog. "Then perhaps
you can help me. I'd like to be in a story."

"By the hair on our chinny-chin-chin,
it's much too tough. You'll never get in,"
said the three little pigs.

So, the little hedgehog went on.

Soon he met ... a
gingerbread man!
"Not *a* gingerbread man!
THE gingerbread man!" he said.
"What! The one in the story?" said
the little hedgehog. "Then perhaps
you can help me. I'd like to be
in a story."

The gingerbread man
shook his head and said,
"I wasn't cut out to be famous.
And being so sweet is no fun.
The moment that everyone
knows who you are,
you spend your whole
life on the run!"

So, the little hedgehog trotted on.

He hadn't gone far before he met...a witch!
"Not *a* witch! *THE* witch!" she snapped.
"w-w-W-What! The one in all the stories?"
said the little hedgehog. "Then perhaps you
can help me. I'd like to be in a story."

The witch cast a beady eye on him and cackled,
"I've been in more stories than you would believe,
I've always a nasty new trick up my sleeve.
I've spells that would make all your prickles turn blue,
so out of my way – or I'll cast
one on
you!"

And the little
hedgehog scuttled
away as fast as his
little legs could
carry him.

No sooner was he out of the forest
than he met…a **princess!**

"Not *a* princess!" she told him. "*THE* princess!"

"What! The one in the stories?" said the little
hedgehog shyly. "Then perhaps you can help me.
I'd like to be in a story."

The princess
gave a **long** sigh.
"Some things, of course, are exciting,
like meeting a prince at the ball.
But a hundred years' sleep,
or kissing a frog,
well, they're not very funny at all!
Take my advice," she said. "Keep out
of stories."

But the little hedgehog went on.

Round the next corner,
he met...three bears!
   "Not *just* three bears," they
said. "*THE* three bears!"
   "What! The ones in the story?"
gasped the little hedgehog. "Then perhaps
you can help me. I'd like to be in a story."

The three bears smiled.
"It's something that everyone dreams of.
And thousands of people have tried.
Take Goldilocks now: she was naughty,
but at least she had looks on her side.
Of course, we can't all be great heroes,
so famous that everyone stares,
and hedgehogs aren't even that cuddly,
but then…

...nothing's as
cuddly as bears."

After tea, the little hedgehog went on his way again.
Suddenly, out pounced… a **big bad wolf!**
"Not *a* big bad wolf! *THE* big bad wolf!" said the wolf.
"What! The one in the stories?" said the little
hedgehog. "Then perhaps you can help me.
I'd like to be in a story."

The wolf smiled slyly.
"I've gobbled up grandmas,
I've wolfed down pigs,
I've stuffed till I'm ready to burst!
Sure, I'll get you into a story...but...

...IT'S
INTO MY
TUMMY
FIRST!"

"So, I rolled up into a ball just like you taught me," the little hedgehog told his mummy, once he was safely back home. "Then...

...the big bad wolf popped me into his mouth...

...BUT I was so prickly he spat me straight out again!

And I ran all
the way home."
  "What a brave little hedgehog!"
said his mummy.
  "Not *a* brave little hedgehog," said the
little hedgehog. "*THE* brave little hedgehog!

Just you wait and see...

...One day there'll be a story...
all about me!"

Meet the Author!

Book Signing Today